SIR JOHN TENNIEL

Alice Through the Pillar-box

For Peter and Jann Blake

Alice Through the Pillar-box

and What She Found There

A Philatelic Phantasy

by Gerald M. King

(with a little assistance from Lewis Carroll and Sir John Tenniel)

Published by Whizzard Press
in association with André Deutsch Ltd., 1978
105 Great Russell Street London W.C.1.

ISBN 233 97059 2

Colour separation by Colour Craftsmen
Printed in Italy by New Interlitho (SPA)
Filmsetting by Baird Harris Filmsetting Limited

Whizzard Press/André Deutsch

King's Preface

July 1965 saw the Centenary of the first publication of Lewis Carroll's 'Alice in Wonderland.' This event, momentous as it was, cut little or no ice with the G.P.O., who seem to insist on persons of note being deceased for at least a hundred years before giving the nod of approval to commemorative issues. Carroll lived until 1898, and not having the patience to wait thirty-odd years, I decided to go it alone and produce a little set of perhaps half a dozen designs. I had not read the book since childhood, and studying it a second time, and examining Tenniel's remarkable illustrations, I was amazed to find so many characters and events leaping from the pages, clamouring for philatelic recognition.

The project then, like Topsy, just grow'd and grow'd! After many months and countless hours of thought, ideas, trial and error, drawing and redrawing, the result is this book.

Every item has its counterpart in philately proper; some blatantly obvious, others perhaps a little more subtle. For example the 'Smiling Boy' health stamp of New Zealand inspired the 'Scowling Boys' issue of Looking Glass Land. The numbers in cross, et cetera, refer to the chess square at which the item was posted, and the hand-stamped chess characters are applied to the covers as the appropriate character's 'receiving or sending marks.'

The details of the printers are of course purely hypothetical and the 'watermarks' can be seen only by moonbeam, and even then, only if you *really* believe in Faerie!

Gerald M. King

Postscript from Paul Jennings

Of *course* we start with a Postscript. As the White Queen remarks, it's a poor sort of memory that only works backwards. Nobody is going to read these merely supererogatory words before looking at the visual contents of this inspired book.

It is a moot point whether there are more philalicists (from the Greek *philos,* 'fond of,' and *Alice)* or philatelists in the world. (Philately, would you believe it, comes from *philos* and *ateleia,* 'exemption from tax,' because the penny post introduced in 1839 by Rowland Hill, setting a standard from which we have been gently declining ever since – it is only the golden Carroll world of innocent nonsense that never declines – ended a system of corrupt farming-out, and of excessive charges, to the second of which ills we have indeed already returned).

Alice has been translated into many languages, including Latin *('Calloo!' clamatque 'Callay!' Vix potuit laetus chorticulare pater),* but of course it is still fundamentally an English work; it was England which, in the very moment of pioneering the Industrial Revolution, the whole whirring, clanking, repetitive, noisy, mass-production, anti-individual, soulless, mechanical (but thank God for penicillin etc.) boring world in which we live (or anyway in which factory workers live), was also pioneering, in the persons of Carroll and Edward Lear, the ever-new, surprising, unpredictable world of Nonsense, in creations with a freedom which makes the later efforts of Surrealists, Dadaists (and, for all I know, Mamaists) look as if they had come from computers. Carroll did not so much create a dream as surrender to one. It just *is.*

But it has been left to a philatelist to do something which any philalicist would have thought impossible. This is an inspired book because it actually adds something to what we all thought was our complete visual perception of Wonderland, as created by Carroll's supporting genius Tenniel (how right that nobody smiles, for instance, except the Cheshire Cat of course. Alice least of all, with that grave, childish, little-old-woman face. Nonsense is serious. Rightly 'how the creatures order one about, and make one repeat lessons' if one doesn't know that soles and eels are cleaned with whiting, and other obvious truths).

Now that Gerald King has done it, we can see the utter inevitability of this book. All inspirations are 'impossible' before someone has them, and blindingly obvious after. In the very year that Carroll made the river trips with Alice Liddell and her sisters (1862), the first journal devoted entirely to postage stamps, *The Monthly Advertiser,* appeared (in Liverpool). The first stamp auctions were held (in Paris) in 1865, the year *Alice in Wonderland* was published. The next year a Frenchman, M.G. Herpin, coined the word *philately.*

It was the golden age of the letter. In the week ending November 24, 1839, just before Rowland Hill's scheme, 1,585,973 letters were sent. In the week ending February 21, 1849, it was 6,849,196. Until our recent dismal past it went on increasing. From great literary figures like Edward Fitzgerald or Ruskin down to

the millions now enabled by the railway to see the sea for the first time ('Alice had been to the seaside once in her life, and had come to the general conclusion that wherever you go to on the English coast, you find a number of bathing-machines in the sea, some children digging in the sand with wooden spades, then a row of lodging-houses, and behind them a railway station'), letters caused people to immortalize their thoughts with some sort of effort, even if only to Wish You Were Here. One thing is certain; there is never going to be a book called *Great Telephone Conversations of the World.*

The whole domestic and public life of the nineteenth century was held in a vast intricate web of correspondence. We shall never see it again. In the 1899 *Strand Magazine* they ran a series called *Stories of the Sanctuary Club,* a kind of Hampstead hydro-cum-health-farm with artificially created climates. One partner, Dr Kort, is rightly suspected of villainy, and when the two honest ones see he has sent a letter when a servant comes at 4.15 p.m. 'for the country letters,' one of them fortunately notes the address (38 Gledham Gardens, South Kensington). The other, told of this around 7 p.m., thinks it may contain the incriminating evidence they need. They get in a cab ('South Kensington, and a sovereign for yourself if you do it in three-quarters of an hour'), put a pouch suspended in the letter-box of the equally villainous recipient by 'almost invisible' black silk threads, wait for the postman to deliver the letter at 9.20 (this is p.m., *the same day),* retrieve it and, too right, it's the beginning of the end for Dr Kort.

Stamps, as philatelists won't need me to tell them (though philalicists may) were originally called 'labels' and the gum was called 'cement' and they weren't adhesive and Henry Archer finally perfected his perforating machine in 1854 (before that you had to cut

them out yourself) and the most beautiful stamps were steel engravings by firms with names like Perkins, Bacon and Petch, and are often most valuable when there is something wrong with them, like an upside-down head, and the 1847 Mauritius 2d which George V bought for £1450 in 1903 was worth £10,000 after the last war and would be nearer £50,000 now, and . . . .

Well, the whole thing is precise, organized, and divinely useless, and highly professional – like good Nonsense writing. It is our good fortune that in Gerald King we have someone who is not only perfectly at home in this world which the late Sir Harold Nicolson dismissed, with the scorn of anyone faced with mysteries from which he is excluded, as 'poring over dismal, murky rectangles', but is clearly a deeply knowledgeable philalicist – not to mention skilled calligraphist and imaginative, witty artist to boot.

What has he been doing all this time? Is he some bearded lecturer, or eccentric old clergyman, retired to Somerset, free at last to complete the majestically authoritative, the definitive work on the stamps of Wonderland? Not a bit of it. It was compiled in the spare time of a busy life as the manager of a betting shop in Islington. This is a district (let me state for overseas philalicists and thesis-writers who must doubtless add this book to the *corpus)* of North London, full of huge container traffic and dusty shop windows containing apparently second-hand dynamos. But its famous inn, the Angel, which has a tube station named after it, was where Tom Paine wrote some of *The Rights of Man.* Charles Lamb lived there. Blake wrote

The fields from Islington to Marylebone,
To Primrose Hill and Saint John's Wood,
Were builded over with pillars of gold
And there Jerusalem's pillars stood.

The golden vision is never far to seek, you see. But it is more likely to come to such a true philalicist as Gerald King than to a mere academic researcher or literary critic. As for the dismal crowd of persons who parrot on with feeble sniggers about the Rev Dodgson's (to them) abnormal interest in little girls (what's wrong with *that?* If they are suggesting he ever did anything but *like* them, let them come out with it, like men. If not, shut up) let me quote one of the more extreme cases.

An American psychologist, Dr Martin Grotjahn, suggested that the drawing of Alice growing was a thinly disguised phallic symbol and went on:

> the process of symbolization becomes more and more retrogressive, and this seems to be true not only of the story of Alice in Wonderland, but quite generally for all later works of Lewis Carroll. Words assume more and more their own meaning and finally have lost their object cathexis like in a schizophrenic psychosis.

Hum. I think you will agree that it is only necessary to glance through this book to see that Gerald King, who wouldn't know an object cathexis if he saw one (and neither would I, thank goodness) is nearer the mark.

He is nearer, among other things, because he is exact, precise, explicit. It has often been pointed out that nursery rhymes are full of numbers – *three* blind mice, *four and twenty* blackbirds, *one* man went to mow, *ten* green bottles, I met a man with *seven* wives. Elizabeth Sewell (well, *she's* a literary critic too, but some of them are useful) in her wonderful book *The Field of Nonsense,** wrote:

> all the finer points of the Nonsense game . . . create a universe which will be logical and orderly, with separate units held together by a strict economy of

**The Field of Nonsense* by Elizabeth Sewell (Chatto & Windus, 1952)

> relations, not subject to dream and disorder with its multiplication of relationships and associations . . . nonsense is so far removed from delirium because it takes infinite pains to prevent associations forming in the mind. From the dangerous ground of stars and diamonds we are led to bats and tea-trays, and so by means of separateness and distinctness . . . we avoid poetry first, then dream, then delirium and madness. Like Hamlet, our proof of sanity in this universe which might so well be lunatic is that we know, not a hawk from a handsaw, but a bat from a tea-tray when the wind is in the right quarter.

Exactly. Even if all you remember of *Alice in Wonderland* is the Mad Hatter's tea-party and the Dormouse, you will appreciate the exquisite aptness of the currency value of the stamps (units of one wink, 40 winks = 1 golden slumber). Who but Gerald King could have imagined, and who could now possibly deny the value to both philatelists and philalicists, of a Jabberwocky Centennial error, printed in reverse on gummed side? (And with what strength of mind has he rightly resisted the temptation to call it a Jabberwocky Centenniel. This is a *serious* book.)

Once the idea had been explained to us, we mere unphilatelic philalicists might have come up with a few ideas about Coronation issues, with all those queens around. But who else would have had that divine idea about the Emergency Inflation Issue, or the Woolwater postmark on the Ship Post from that boat with the Sheep, or....

but look for yourselves, and you will, like me, find there is only one adjective for it. It is frabjous.

The William Unready Envelope.

Wonderland Currency ~ 40 Winks = 1 Golden Slumber.

First Definitive Issue.

Printed by Dodo, Lory & Co. Watermk: Daisy Chain.

Imperf. Perf 10¾.

Alice was beginning to get very tired of sitting by her sister on the bank, and of having nothing to do . . . she was considering whether the pleasure of making a daisy-chain would be worth the trouble of getting up and picking the daisies, when suddenly a White Rabbit with pink eyes ran close by her. There was nothing *very* remarkable in that; nor did Alice think it so *very* much out of the way to hear the Rabbit say to itself "Oh, dear! Oh, dear! I shall be too late!". . . but when the Rabbit actually took a watch out of it's waistcoat-pocket and looked at it, and hurried on, she started to her feet – for it flashed through her mind that she had never before seen a rabbit with either a waistcoat-pocket, or a watch to take out of it, and burning with curiosity she ran after it and was just in time to see it pop down a large rabbit-hole under the hedge.

In another moment down went Alice after it, never once considering how in the world she was to get out again . . . .

"Curiouser and curiouser!" cried Alice. "Now I'm opening out like the largest telescope that ever was."

"Goodbye feet!" for when she looked down at her feet – they seemed to be almost out of sight they were getting so far off.

"Oh! my poor little feet! – I wonder who will put on your shoes and stockings for you now, I'm sure I won't be able.

I shall be too far off to ever trouble about you . . . you must manage the best way you can."

Emergency Inflation Issue.

Watermark: EAT ME. several times on each portion of the stamp.

A Cover from Alice to her right foot: with transit mark.

..."But I must be kind to them" thought Alice, "or perhaps they won't walk the way I want to go! Let me see – I'll give them a new pair of boots every Christmas."

And she went on planning to herself how she would manage it. "They must go by the Carrier," she thought; "and how funny it will seem, sending presents to ones own feet! And how odd the directions will look!"

Olympic Games & First Running of Caucus Race

When they had been running half an hour or so, the Dodo suddenly called out "The race is over!" and they all crowded round it, panting and asking "But who has won?" At last the Dodo said "Everybody has won, and all must have prizes". . . .

. . . "What else have you got in your pocket?" he went on, turning to Alice. "Only a thimble" said she, sadly. "Hand it over here" said the Dodo. Then they all crowded round her once more, while the Dodo solemnly presented the thimble, saying "We beg your acceptance of this elegant thimble. And when it had finished this short speech, they all cheered.

A cover to Alice's cat Dinah ~ Apparently lost in transit... subsequently sent to the Dead Letter Office.

"I wish I hadn't mentioned Dinah!" she said to herself in a melancholy tone. "Nobody seems to like her down here. Oh my dear Dinah! I wonder if I shall ever see you again!"

Centenary of Discovery of Wonderland

Suddenly she came upon a little three-legged table, all made of solid glass; there was nothing on it except a tiny golden key . . . . she then came upon a low curtain she had not noticed before, and behind it was a little door about fifteen inches high. Alice opened the door and looked into the loveliest garden you ever saw . . . . .

. . . "Oh, so Bill's got to come down the chimney, has he?" said Alice to herself. "This fireplace is narrow, to be sure, but I think I can kick a little!" She gave one sharp kick and waited to see what would happen next.... at last came a feeble, squeaking voice saying: "All I knows is, something comes at me like a jack-in-the-box, and up I goes like a sky-rocket!"

Special Space Issue. Bill 1. First Lizard in Space.

Centenary of Citizen's Advice Bureau

Recess-printed by Old Father William & Son.

Watermark ~ Smoke Rings

Advertisement on back.

She stretched herself up on tiptoe and peeped over the edge of the mushroom, and her eyes immediately met those of a large blue Caterpillar that was sitting on the top with its arms folded, quietly smoking a large hookah and taking not the smallest notice of her or of anything else .... "Repeat 'You Are Old, Father William' " said the Caterpillar. Alice folded her hands, and began ....

... "You are old" said the youth, "as I mentioned before
And have grown most uncommonly fat;
Yet you turned a back somersault in at the door-
Pray, what is the reason for that?"
"In my youth" said the sage, as he shook his grey locks,
"I kept all my limbs very supple
By the use of this ointment ~ one shilling a box-
Allow me to sell you a couple!"

Royal Household Official

. . . . . The Fish-Footman began by producing from under his arm a great letter nearly as big as himself; and this he handed to the Frog-Footman, saying in a solemn tone: "For the Duchess ~ ~ an invitation from the Queen to play croquet."

Child Welfare Week

Printed by Pigg, Pepper & Co. Wm. Frying-pan

The door led to a large kitchen which was full of smoke from one end to the other; the Duchess was sitting on a three-legged stool in the middle, nursing a baby; the cook was leaning over the fire stirring a large cauldron . . . .

National Wildlife Week

Recess-printed by Pigg, Pepper & Co.

Early state of the plate - cat fully visible.

Worn plate. cat hardly visible.

Said Alice ~ "I wish you wouldn't keep appearing and disapp-
-earing like that ~ you make one quite giddy!" "All right" said the Cat, and this time it vanished quite slowly, beginning with the tail, and ending with the grin, which remained for some time after the rest of it had gone . . . . .

Umpteenth Centenary of Mad Tea-party.

Drawn on treacle by Elsie, Lacey & Tilley. Wink Raven/Writing Desk.

There was a table set out under a tree in front of the house, and the March Hare and the Hatter were having tea at it; a Dormouse was sitting bet-
-ween them, fast asleep, and the other two were resting their elbows on it and talking over it's head.

Hattersville to Muchness, with Receiving Mark

"What day of the month is it?" asked the Hatter, turning to Alice. She considered a little, and then said "the fourth". "Two days wrong!" sighed the Hatter. "I told you butter wouldn't suit the works!"

. . . .

. . . . "well, I'd hardly finished the first verse when the Queen jumped up and bawled out "He's murdering the time! Off with his head!" and ever since, he won't do a thing I ask. It's always six o'clock now!"

. . . .

"Once upon a time, began the Dormouse, there were three little sisters and their names were Elsie, Lacie and Tillie, and they lived at the bottom of a well—" . . . . "they drew all manner of things - everything that begins with an "M", such as mouse-traps, and the moon, and memory, and muchness" . . .

Botanical Congress.

Engraved on Batter Pudding. W'mark D.D.T. & Spray.

A large rose-tree stood near the entrance of the garden; the roses growing on it were white; but there were three gardeners busily painting them red. Alice thought this a very curious thing. "Would you tell me," she asked "why are you painting those roses?" Five and Seven said nothing but Two said "Why the fact is, you see, this here ought to have been a red rose-tree, but we put in a white one by mistake; and if the Queen was to find out, we should all have our heads chopped off, you know."

At this moment, Five, who had been anxiously looking across the garden, called out "The Queen! The Queen!" and the three gardeners instantly threw themselves flat on their faces.

"Get up!" shouted the Queen, in a shrill, loud voice, and the gardeners instantly jumped up and began bowing to the King, the Queen, the Royal children, and everybody else. "Leave off that!" screamed the Queen, and then, turning to the rose tree, she went on "What HAVE you been doing here?" ...."May it please your Majesty, we were trying to ~" "I SEE!" bellowed the Queen, who had mean-while been examining the roses. "OFF WITH THEIR HEADS!"

(.... Owing to the need for a new value, and due to the dire shortage of Batter Pudding, the 3 wink was beheaded / bisected by the Royal Executioner!)

Royal Visit.

"You can't think how glad I am to see you again, you dear old thing!" said the Duchess, as she tucked her arm affectionately into Alice's, and they walked off together. She had quite forgotten the Duchess by this time and was a little startled to hear her voice close to her ear.... "Thinking again?" the Duchess asked, with another dig of her sharp little chin. "I've a right to think" said Alice, sharply. "Just as much right" said the Duchess, "as pigs have to fly; and the m— ' but here her voice died away, even in the middle of her favourite word "moral", and she began to tremble. There stood the Queen in front of them, with a frown like a thunderstorm... "Now I give you fair warning- either you or your head must be off! and that in about half no time! Take your choice!" The Duchess took her choice, and was gone in a moment.

Umpteenth Renewal of Olympic Games.
Printed by Mocke, Turtell & Co. Wmk: Gryphon.

"Get to your places!" shouted the Queen in a voice of thunder, and people began running about in all directions, tumbling up against each other. Alice thought she had never seen such a curious Croquet-ground in her life; it was all ridges and furrows; the balls were live hedgehogs, the mallets live Flamingoes; and the soldiers had to double themselves up to make the arches. The players all played at once, without waiting for turns; quarreling all the while, and fighting for the hedgehogs; and soon the Queen was in a furious passion, and went stamping about shouting "OFF WITH HIS HEAD!" about once every minute.....

... They had not gone far before they saw the Mock Turtle, sitting sad and lonely on a little ledge of rock, sighing as if his heart would break....
... "Once", the Mock Turtle sighed; "Once I was a real Turtle"......

Mourning Cover ... in respect for the fate of the Oysters.

Festival of Oceanography.

Watermarks: Teardrops (Turtle) and "HJCKRRH" (Gryphon).

"You can have no idea," said the Mock Turtle, "what a delightful thing a Lobster Quadrille is." "It must be a very pretty dance," said Alice.
"Would you like to see a little of it?" asked the Mock Turtle.
"Very much indeed!" said Alice.

Centenary of Lobster Quadrille.

"Stand up and repeat '*Tis the voice of the sluggard*'," said the Gryphon, but her head was so full of the Lobster Quadrille that the words came very queer indeed.

"'Tis the voice of the Lobster; I heard him declare,
"You have baked me too brown, I must sugar my hair."
As a duck with its eyelids, so he with his nose
Trims his belt and his buttons, and turns out his toes.
When the sands are all dry, he is gay as a lark,
And will talk in contemptuous tones of the Shark:
But, when the tide rises and sharks are around,
His voice has a timid and tremulous sound.'

Centenary of the Trial of The Knave of Hearts
Wmk: Multiple Jam Tart

The King and Queen of Hearts were seated on their throne when Alice arrived, with a great crowd assembled around them ~ all sorts of little birds and beasts, as well as the whole pack of cards; the Knave was standing before them in chains, with a soldier on each side to guard him; and near the King was the White Rabbit with a trumpet in one hand and a scroll of parchment in the other. "Herald, read the accusation!" said the King. On this the White Rabbit blew three blasts on his trumpet, unrolled the scroll of parchment and read as follows:

'The Queen of Hearts, she made some tarts, all on a summer's day'
The Knave of Hearts, he stole those tarts, and took them quite away.'

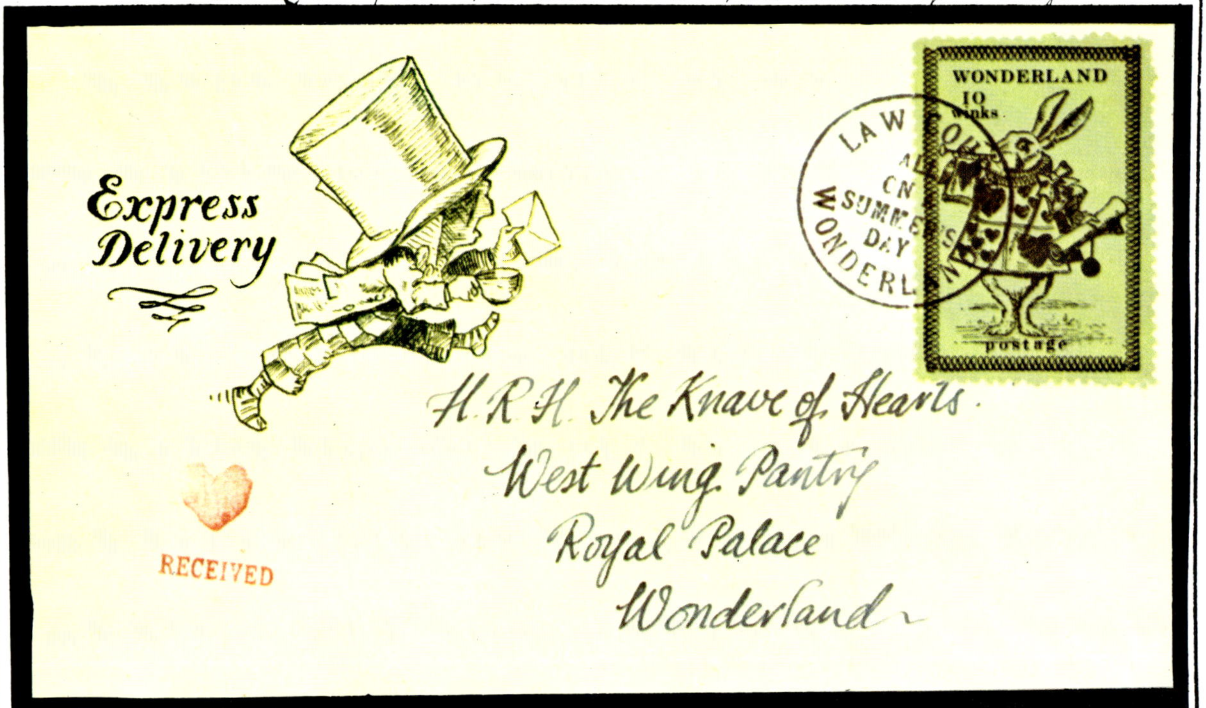

Cover to the Knave of Hearts which contained the summons to court.

Looking-glass Land

Dramatis Personae

White			Red
Tweedledee	Daisy	Daisy	Humpty Dumpty
Unicorn	Haigha	Messenger	Carpenter
Sheep	Oyster	Oyster	Walrus
W. Queen	Lily	Tiger-lily	Red Queen
W. King	Fawn	Rose	Red King
Aged Man	Oyster	Oyster	Crow
W. Knight	Hatta	Frog	Red Knight
Tweedledum	Daisy	Daisy	Lion

The William Unready Envelope.

1871

International Chess Conference
Engraved on Ivory by N. Passant. Wink-Check

"They don't keep this room so tidy as the other" thought Alice to herself, as she noticed several of the chessmen down in the hearth among the cinders; but in another moment, with a little "Oh!" of surprise, she was down on her hands and knees watching them. The chessmen were walking about two by two!

"Here are the Red King and Queen" Alice said, "and there are the White King and Queen sitting on the edge of the shovel ~ and here are two Castles walking arm-in-arm . . ."

Jabberwocky Centennial.

Engraved on tulgey wood: Recess; A. Van der Snatch.

Watermark: Vorpal Sword.

There was a book lying near Alice on the table; she turned over the leaves to find some part that she could read; "For it's all in some language I don't know" she said to herself.

It was like this . . .

JABBERWOCKY . . . .

'Twas brillig and the slithy toves
Did gyre and gimble in the wabe;
All mimsy were the borogoves,
And the mome raths outgrabe.

Error. Printed in reverse on gummed side.

Jabberwocky Centennial

'Twas brillig, and the slithy toves
Did gyre and gimble in the wabe;
All mimsy were the Borogoves,
And the Mome Raths outgrabe.

"Beware the Jabberwock, my son!
The jaws that bite, the claws that catch!
Beware the Jub-jub bird, and shun
The frumious Bandersnatch!"

He took his vorpal sword in hand:
Long time the manxome foe he sought ~
So rested he by the tum-tum tree,
And stood awhile in thought.

And, as in uffish thought he stood,
The Jabberwock, with eyes of flame,
Came whiffling through the Tulgey Wood
And burbled as it came!

One two! One two! and through and through
The vorpal blade went snicker-snack!
He left it dead ~ and with its head
He went galumphing back.

"And hast thou slain the Jabberwock?"
Come to my arms my beamish boy!
O frabjous day! Callooh! Callay!"
He chortled in his joy.

'Twas brillig, and the slithy toves
Did gyre and gimble in the wabe;
All mimsy were the Borogoves,
And the Mome Raths outgrabe.

Variety:~
Imperf between
knees!

Second Botanical Congress.

Printed by the Luke Inglis Printing Works.

Watermark : Butterflies.

"Are there any more people in the garden besides me?" Alice asked. "There's one other flower in the garden that can move about like you, but she's redder, and her petals are shorter". "She's coming!" the Larkspur cried, "I can hear her footsteps, thump! thump! along the gravel-walk!" Alice looked round eagerly, and saw that it was the Red Queen . . . . .

Express Delivery

. . "You can be the White Queen's pawn, if you like; and you're in the second square to begin with; when you get to the eighth square ~ you'll be a Queen ~" just at that moment, somehow or other, they began to run . . . . .

Looking-Glass Insects

Watermark: DDT & Spray.

Rocking-horsefly.

Snap-dragon-fly.

Bread and Butterfly

Looking-Glass Railway Post.

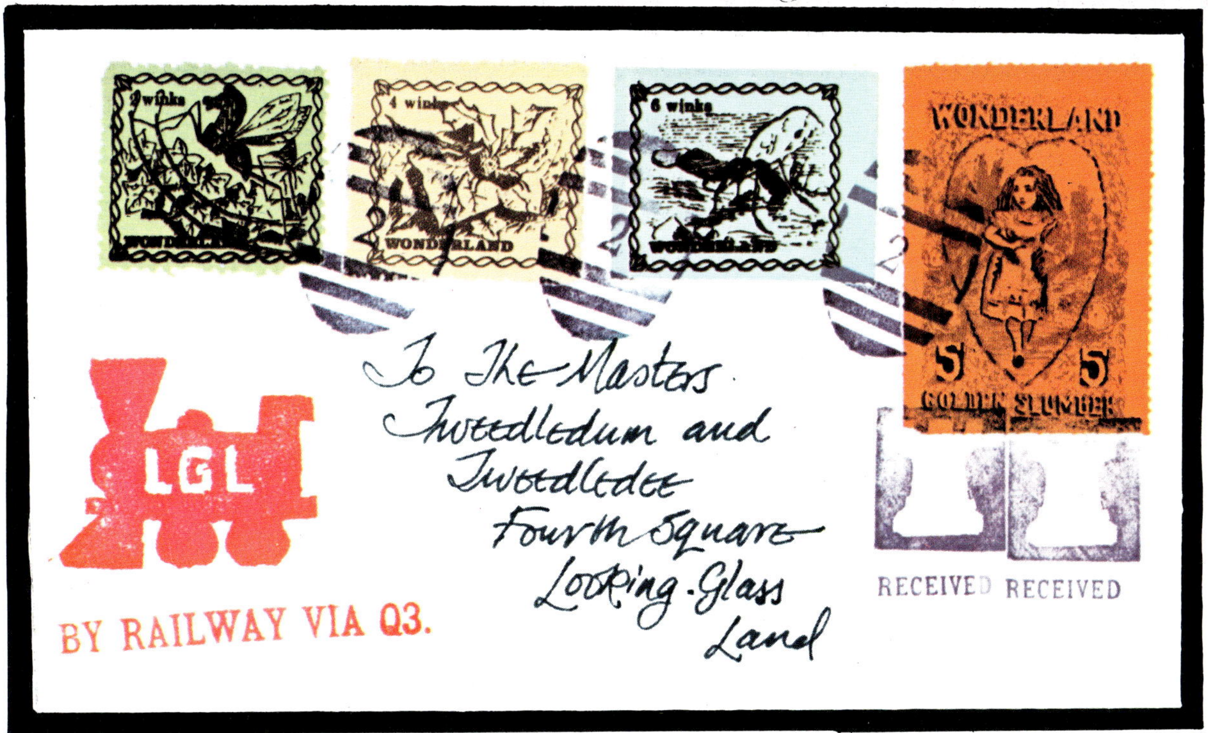

"You'll go *very* quickly through the Third Square – by Railway, I should think – and you'll find yourself in the Fourth Square in no time. Well, *that* square belongs to Tweedledum and Tweedledee . . ."

Railway Post

"Tickets please!" said the Guard, putting his head in at the window. "Now then, show your ticket, child!" "I'm afraid I haven't got one," Alice said, "there wasn't a ticket office where I came from."

"Don't make excuses," said the Guard; "you should have bought one from the Engine-driver." And once more the chorus of voices went on: "The man that drives the engine. Why, the smoke alone is worth a thousand pounds a puff!" All this time the Guard was looking at her, first through a telescope, then through a microscope, and then through an opera-glass. At last he said "You're travelling the wrong way!"

UNDELIVERED FOR REASON STATED —
Going the wrong way.

Marked on reverse of cover

Health Stamps
Printed by Luke Inglis Printing Works
Watermark : Rattle

They were standing under a tree, each with an arm around the other's neck and Alice knew which was which in a moment, because one of them had "Dum" embroidered on his collar, and the other, "Dee". . . . "I was wondering," Alice said, very politely "which is the best way out of this wood: it's getting so dark. Would you tell me, please?" But the fat little men only looked at each other and grinned. . . "What shall I repeat to her?" said Tweedledee, ignoring Alice's question. "'The Walrus and the Carpenter' is the longest" Tweedledum replied, and Dee began instantly. . . .

"The sun was shining on the sea,
Shining with all his might:
He did his very best to make
The billows smooth and bright –
And this was odd, because it was
The middle of the night."

National Education.
Engraved on Sealing-wax.
Printed by Wool, Water & Co
Watermark : Oyster-shells
(out of season)

"The time has come, the Walrus said,
To talk of many things:
Of shoes, and ships, and sealing-wax:
Of cabbages – and kings –
And why the sea is boiling hot –
And whether pigs have wings."

Airmail

A Letter from T'dum & T'dee bearing "their stamp with "Monstrous Crow" obliteration.

. . . Just then flew down a monstrous Crow,
As black as a tar-barrel;
Which frightened both the heroes so,
They quite forgot their quarrel.
. . . .

It was getting dark so suddenly that Alice thought there must be a thunderstorm coming on. "What a thick black cloud that is!" she said. "And how fast it comes! Why, I do believe it has wings!"

"It's the crow!" Tweedledum cried out in a shrill voice of alarm: and the two brothers took to their heels and were out of sight in a moment . . . .

Ship Letter

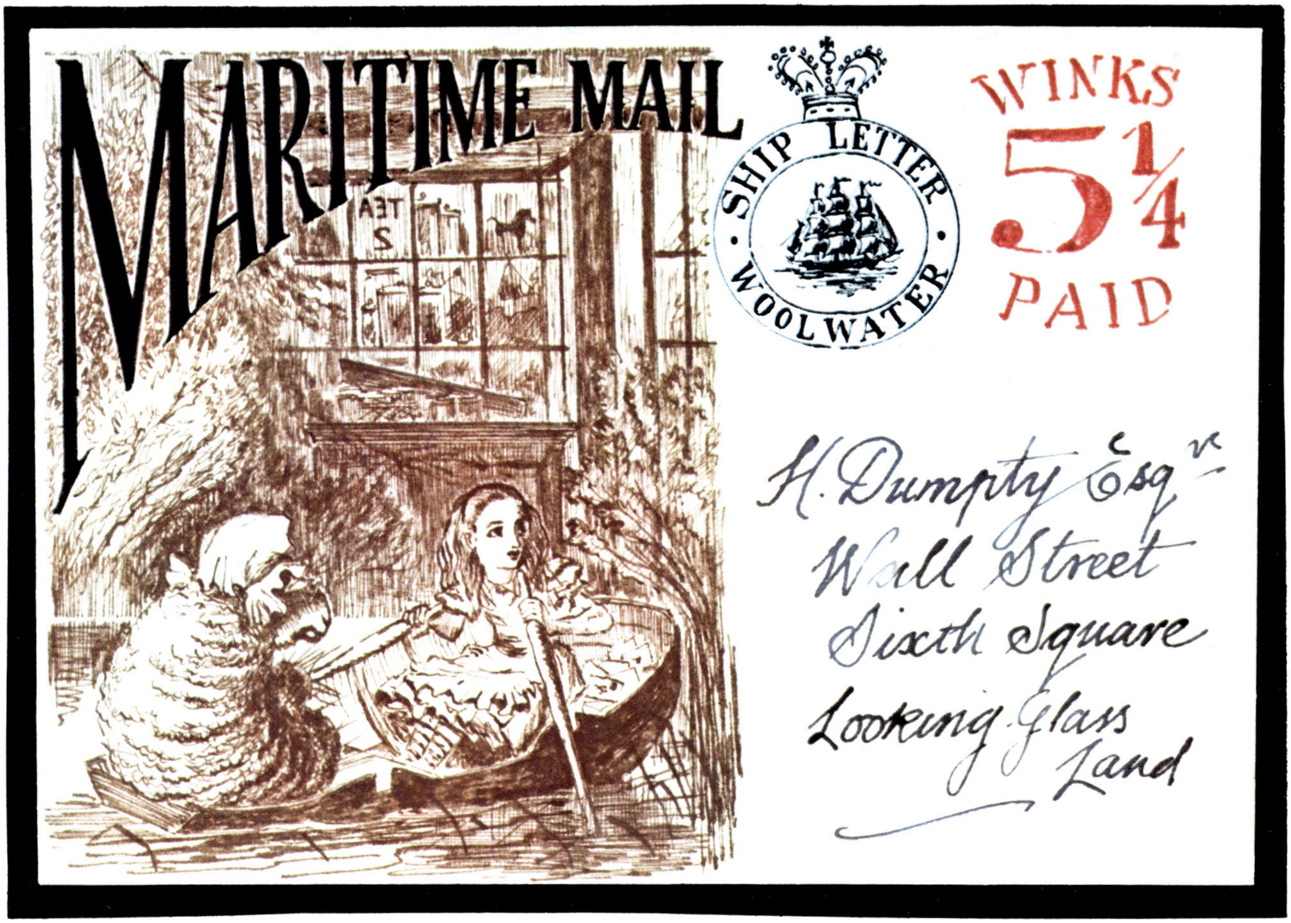

"Can you row?" the Sheep asked, handing her a pair of knitting needles as she spoke. "Yes, a little - but not on land - and not with needles" ~ Alice was beginning to say, when suddenly the needles turned to oars in her hands and she found herself in a little boat, gliding along between the banks. "Are there many crabs here?" asked Alice. "Crabs and all sorts of things" said the Sheep: "plenty of choice, only make up your mind. Now, what *do* you want to buy?" ~ the oars, the boat and the river had vanished all in a moment, and she was back again in the little dark shop.

"I should like to buy an egg, please" she said timidly. "How do you sell them?" "Five-pence-farthing for one, twopence for two" the Sheep replied. "Only you *must* eat them both, if you buy two."

Private Messenger Post

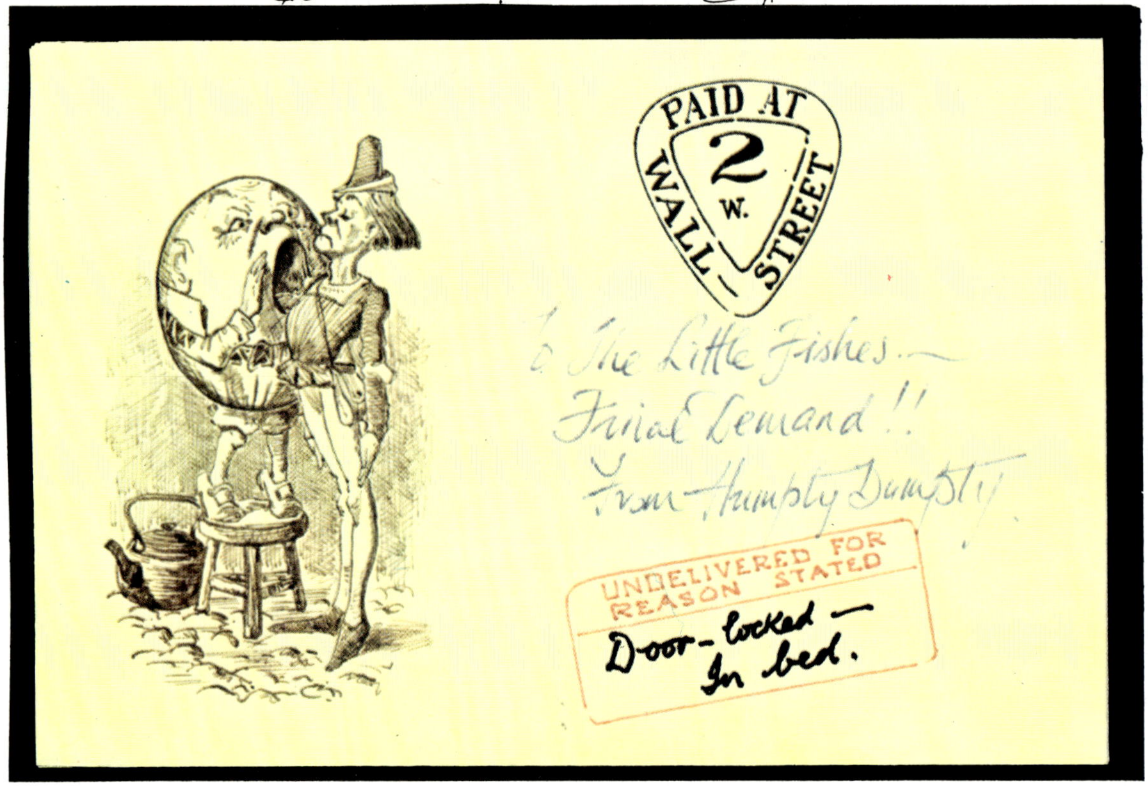

'I sent a message to the fish:
I told them "This is what I wish."

The little fishes of the sea,
They sent an answer back to me.

The little fishes answer was
"We cannot do it, Sir, because —"

I sent to them again to say
"It will be better to obey."

I told them once, I told them twice:
They would not listen to advice.

Then someone came to me and said
"The little fishes are in bed."

I said to him, I said it plain,
"Then you must wake them up again!"

I said it very loud and clear;
I went and shouted in his ear.'

But he was very stiff and proud;
He said "You needn't shout so loud!"

I took a corkscrew from the shelf:
I went to wake them up myself.

And when I found the door was shut,
I tried to turn the handle, but —'

Military Post

. . . . at this moment a heavy crash shook the forest from end to end. The next moment soldiers came running through the wood, first in twos and threes, then ten or twenty together, and at last in such crowds that they seemed to fill the whole forest. Alice was very glad to get into an open space, where she found the White King busily writing in his mem-orandum book. "I've sent them all!" the King cried, on seeing Alice, "Did you happen to meet any soldiers, my dear, as you came through the wood?" "Yes, I did" said Alice, "several thousand, I should think."

"Four thousand, two hundred and seven, that's the exact number," the King said, referring to his book. "I couldn't send all the horses, because two of them are wanted for the game. I haven't sent the messengers either, they're both gone to the town. Just look along the road and tell me if you can see either of them."

Political Prisoner's Relief Fund

Sold at half face value: the other ¼ wink being charged to Hatta, therefore relieving him of a quarter wink!.. Watermark: jam (on every other stamp!) ... "What sort of things do you remember best?" Alice ventured to ask. "Oh, things that happened the week after next", the White Queen replied. "For instance now, there's the King's Messenger. He's in prison now, being punished; and the trial doesn't begin 'til next Wednesday, and of course the crime comes last of all!"

Hare Mail. (Watermark: Ham Sandwich)

Alice was still looking intently along the road. "I see somebody now!" she exclaimed at last. "But he's coming very slowly – and what curious attitudes he goes into!" For the Messenger kept skipping up and down, wriggling like an eel as he came along, with his great hands spread out like fans on each side ....

Haremail Cover with Postage Due (Watermark Hay)

"He's an Anglo-Saxon Messenger" said the King, "and those are Anglo-Saxon attitudes. He only does them when he's happy. His name is Haigha; the other Messenger is called Hatta. I must have two, you know, to come and go. One to come and one to go."

At this moment the Messenger arrived; he was far too much out of breath to say a word; and could only wave his hands about and make the most fearful faces at the poor King....

"When you've got your breath back, you may tell us what's been happening in the town." "I'll whisper it" said the Messenger, putting his hands to his mouth in the shape of a trumpet, and stooping so as to get close to the King's ear. However, instead of whispering, he simply shouted at the top of his voice "They're at it again!"

A Letter to Messrs. Lion & Unicorn, Showing Usual Transits.

'The Lion and the Unicorn were fighting for the crown;
The Lion beat the Unicorn all round the town.
Some gave them white bread and some gave them brown;
Some gave them plum-cake and drummed them out of town.

"What a fight we might have for the crown *now*!" the Unicorn said, looking slyly up at the crown, which the poor King was nearly shaking off his head, as he trembled so much. "I should win easy" said the Lion. "I'm not so sure of that!" said the Unicorn. "Why, I beat you all round the town, you chicken!" the Lion replied angrily. Here the King interrupted, to prevent the quarrel going on. "All round the town?" he asked. "That's a good long way. Did you go by the Old Bridge, or the Market-place? You get the best view by the Old Bridge." "I'm sure I don't know", the Lion growled, as he lay down again. "There was too much dust to see anything!"

Umpteenth Anniversary of Universal Postal Union.

Photo: Whytbread & Browne. Watermark: Plum Cake.

Without overprint.

"Who are at it again?" Alice ventured to ask. "Why, the Lion and the Unicorn, of course" said the King. "Fighting for the crown?" "Yes, to be sure; and the best of the joke is that it's MY crown all the while!" "And does the one that wins get the crown? Alice asked. "Dear me, no!" said the King. "The very idea!"

Overprinted "WAR TAX"

Road Safety Week.

Lithographed by The Aged Aged Man

Watermark: Haddock's Eyes.

Whenever the horse stopped (which it did very often), he fell off in front; and when it went on again (which it generally did rather suddenly), he fell off behind. Otherwise, he kept on rather well, apart from falling off sideways......

Freedom From Hunger

Engraved on Parsley Sauce by Kaye, Terring & Co. Watermark: Multiple Knife & Fork.

The leg of mutton got up in the dish and made a little bow to Alice, and she returned the bow not knowing whether to be frightened or amused. "May I cut you a slice?" she asked, taking up the knife and fork and looking from one Queen to the other. "Certainly not!" the Red Queen said, very decidedly. "It isn't etiquette to cut anyone you've been introduced to. Remove the joint!" And the waiters carried it off, and brought a large plum-pudding in it's place....

Variety: Cracked Plate.

Coronation Issue.

Watermark: Crown over A.

"And now for the last brook and to be a Queen! How grand it sounds!" "The Eighth Square at last!" she cried as she bounded over and threw herself down on a lawn as soft as moss, with little flowers dotted all about it. "Oh, how glad I am to be here! And what is this on my head?" she exclaimed, as she put her hands up to find something very heavy that fitted tight round her head. It was a GOLDEN CROWN.

The End

Definitive Issue - Second Printing.
Rouletted.

Early State of Plate.
Clear Impression.

Worn Plate.
Faint Impression.

Tete - beche

Very worn plate.

Definitive Issue ~ Third Printing
Imperforate

Definitive Issue - Third Printing
Imprint Sheets of 9
(Dodo, Lory & Co)

Head inverted

Block showing the two types of ½ wink.

Diagonal fraction-bar

Horizontal fraction-bar.

LEWIS CARROLL